PUBLISHER'S NOTE

alter Crane was a multi-talented artist, a painter in oils and watercolor and a calligrapher, as well as a designer of wallpapers, stained glass, ceramics, pottery, and textiles. It is for his illustrations of children's books, however, that he is best known. He was born in Liverpool in 1845, the son of portrait painter and illustrator Thomas Crane. Although young Walter had little formal schooling, he greatly benefited from the time he spent in his father's studio, where his artistic talent was encouraged as he sketched, painted, and began illustrating projects under the guidance of the elder Crane.

William James Linton, a noted wood engraver of the mid-nineteenth century, offered the teenaged Walter an apprenticeship. Now the boy began to truly develop his craft, studying the works of artists such as the Pre-Raphaelites Dante Gabriel Rossetti and John Everett Millais. Crane was greatly influenced by these artists, whose depiction of medieval subject matter made a deep impression on him. After several years with Linton, Crane met Edmund Evans, a printer who was engaged in the development of processes for color printing. Crane's illustrations seemed ideal for the new color printing because of their well-defined images, an outgrowth of Crane's exposure to Japanese woodblock prints, from which he had absorbed the stylistic use of strong outlines and flat areas of color. By the time he was in his twenties, Crane was designing, illustrating, and occasionally providing text for inexpensive children's story books (called "toy" books). These books, such as *A Song of Sixpence, Goody Two Shoes,* and *Baby's Own Alphabet,* were extremely popular with Victorian audiences. In addition, Crane wrote and illustrated over two dozen books for his own children.

Despite the rapid advances in science, technology, and industrialization that marked the era, Victorians were drawn to images of the gentler, magical world of fantasy and mythology (popularized in the art of the Pre-Raphaelites and others). Many such images already existed in the imagination of British artists and writers, notably Shakespeare's *A Midsummer Night's Dream* and *The Tempest.* W.B. Yeats contributed to the field with his *Fairy and Folk Tales of Ireland* (1892). George Cruikshank produced a *Fairy Library,* the first volume appearing in 1853. Richard Doyle illustrated *The Fairy Ring* (1846) and *In Fairyland* (1870). Walter Crane used images of fairyland in many ways: He produced designs in watercolors for fairy costumes for a Christmas pageant; he illustrated Oscar Wilde's collection of tales, *The Happy Prince* (1888) and Edmund Spenser's *The Fairie Queene* (1894); he dedicated to Charles Darwin his work *The First of May, A Fairy Masque* (1881).

Flora's Feast, originally published in 1889, is, perhaps, Crane's best-known work. Flower fairies were favorite subjects of Victorian art and literature, for the nineteenth-century interest in folklore found an apt subject in flowers; ancient beliefs and symbolism were rife among the blooms and blossoms.

The Rev. Hilderic Friend's two-volume work, *Flower Lore* (1884), provided much material for study, as did Thomas Keightley's *The Fairy Mythology* (1828). The 40 color illustrations reproduced in Crane's *Flora's Feast* depict a procession of flowers—appearing in the sequence that they would bloom—as Queen Flora summons them from their "sullen" winter sleep. From the first Snowdrops to spring Hyacinths, summer Lilies, autumn Hollyhocks, and winter's Christmas Rose, the personifications are designed to charm the reader. Crane provides an array of costumes—fanciful versions of petals and leaves; loose, flowing classical attire; late Victorian and medieval dress styles; and even a suit of armor. Crane includes some stunningly original touches of whimsy: the gigantic daisy "eyes" of the Oxeye; the ferocious tigers leaping from the Tiger lilies; the cow's head suspended from the narrow Cowslip stem; and the mace-wielding black knight who suggests the prickly Thorn.

Walter Crane remained one of the outstanding creators of Victorian children's literature until his death in 1915.

FLORA'S FEAST

A Fairy's Festival of Flowers in Full Color

by

Walter Crane

DOVER PUBLICATIONS, INC.
Mineola, New York

Published in Canada by General Publishing Company, Ltd., 895 Don Mills Road, 400-2 Park Centre, Toronto, Ontario M3C 1W3.
Published in the United Kingdom by David & Charles, Brunel House, Forde Close, Newton Abbot, Devon TQ12 4PU.

Bibliographical Note

This Dover edition, first published in 2002, is an unabridged republication of the work published by Cassell & Company, Limited, London, Paris, New York & Melbourne, in 1889 under the title *Flora's Feast: A Masque of Flowers.* A Publisher's Note has been specially prepared for this edition.

Library of Congress Cataloging-in-Publication Data

Crane, Walter, 1845–1915.
Flora's Feast: A Fairy's Festival of Flowers / Walter Crane.
p. cm.
Originally published: Flora's feast. London ; New York : Cassell & Co., 1889.
ISBN 0-486-41858-8 (pbk.)
1. Crane, Walter, 1845–1915. 2. Fairies in art. I. Title.

NC242.C67 A4 2002
741.6'42'092—dc21

2001047220

Manufactured in the United States of America
Dover Publications, Inc., 31 East 2nd Street, Mineola, N.Y. 11501

[original title page]

The sullen winter nearly spent,
Queen Flora to her garden went,
To call the flowers from their long sleep,
The year's glad festivals to keep:

And one by one each
making bold
Their silken vesture
to unfold,
And peeping forth to meet
the sun,
The long procession is begun:-

The Snowdrops first upon the scene,
White-crested braved King Frost's demesne:

The little Crocus
reaches up
To catch a sunbeam
in his cup.

The Daffodil his trumpet blows,
And after Spring a-
hunting
goes.

Anemones rode out the gale,
Frail Wind-flowers flutter'd,
red & pale:

The Violet, and the Primrose dame,
With modest mien but hearts
aflame,

Green-kirtled from the brooklet's fold,
The rustic maid Marsh-Marigold:

The "Lady smocks all silver white"
The milkmaids of the meadows
bright,

Where shining Buttercups abound,
Among the Cowslips on the
ground.

Here Lords and Ladies of the wood,
With shaking spear, and riding-
hood:

Black knight-at-arms, the white-plumed Thorn;
In pomp the Crown-Imperial borne.

While Tulips lift the banner red,
Or fill the cups with
fire instead.

Sweet Hyacinths their bells did ring,
To swell the music of the Spring.

With blazoned
pennons from
each spear,
The Iris
and the
Flag ap-
-pear

Sweet masking May, in white or red,
Her snowy cloud of blossom spread.

And Chaucer's Daisy small & sweet—
"Si douce est la Margarete."

The little Lilies of the Vale,
White ladies delicate & pale;

Great Peonies in crimson pride,
And budding ones
in green that
hide:

Fair Columbines that drew the car
Of Venus
from her distant
star:

And Love's own flower the blushing Rose,
The Queen of all the garden close:

And Roses from the hedgerow wild,
Behind their thorns that faintly smiled.

And from the cressy brook's green side,
"Forget-me-not", a small voice cried.

Here stately Lilies, pale and proud,
In vesture pure as summer cloud;

Or, burning like an orange flame,
With torches borne aloft
they came.

The Monk that wears the hood of blue,
The Bells of Canterbury, too:

Wide Oxeyes in the meads
that gaze

On scarlet Poppy-heads a-blaze:

Ere Evening Primrose
lights her lamp,
A beacon to the garden camp:

When Lilies of the day are done,
And sunk the golden westering sun.

Fresh Pinks cast incense on the air,
In fluttering garments fringed & rare.

Their cousin from the corn in blue;
Corn Marigold of golden hue.

The fond Convolvulus still clings,
The Honeysuckle spreads his wings.

The Hollyhock his standard high,
Rears proudly to the autumn sky.

The blazing Sunflower, black and bold,
Burns yet to win the sun-set's gold,

That, reddening on the Triton's spear,
Foretells the waning of the year.

Then lilies, turned to Tigers, blaze
Amid the garden's tangled maze

There still in triumph, stiff with gold,
The rich Chrysanthemums unfold.

Ere doth the floral pageant close
With one last flower –
a Christmas Rose.

THE-END.